THE RED

By

H.G. WELLS

British Library Cataloguing-in-Publication Data
A catalogue record for this book is available from
the British Library

H. G. WELLS

Herbert George Wells was born in Bromley, England in 1866. He apprenticed as a draper before becoming a pupil-teacher at Midhurst Grammar School in West Sussex. Some years later, Wells won a scholarship to the School of Science in London, where he developed a strong interest in biology and evolution, founding and editing the *Science Schools Journal*. However, he left before graduating to return to teaching, and began to focus increasingly on writing. His first major essay on science, 'The Rediscovery of the Unique', appeared in 1891. However, it was in 1895 that Wells seriously established himself as a writer, with the publication of the now iconic novel, *The Time Machine*.

Wells followed *The Time Machine* with the equally well-received *War of the Worlds* (1898), which proved highly popular in the USA, and was serialized in the magazine *Cosmopolitan*. Around the turn of the century, he also began to write extensively on politics, technology and the future, producing works *The Discovery of the Future* (1902) and *Mankind in the Making* (1903). An active socialist, in 1904 Wells joined the Fabian Society, and his 1905 book *A Modern Utopia* presented a vision of a socialist society founded on reason and compassion. Wells also penned a range of successful comic novels, such as *Kipps* (1905) and *The History of Mr Polly* (1910).

Wells' 1920 work, *The Outline of History*, was penned in response to the Russian Revolution, and declared that world would be improved by education, rather than revolution. It made Wells one of the most important political thinkers of the twenties and thirties, and he began to write for a number of journals and newspapers, even travelling to Russia to lecture Lenin and Trotsky on social reform. Appalled by the carnage of World War II, Wells began to work on a project dealing with the perils of nuclear war, but died before completing it. He is now regarded as one of the greatest science-fiction writers of all time, and an important political thinker.

THE RED ROOM

"I can assure you," said I, "that it will take a very tangible ghost to frighten me." And I stood up before the fire with my glass in my hand.

"It is your own choosing," said the man with the withered arm, and glanced at me askance.

"Eight-and-twenty years," said I, "I have lived, and never a ghost have I seen as yet."

The old woman sat staring hard into the fire, her pale eyes wide open. "Ay," she broke in; "and eight-and-twenty years you have lived and never seen the likes of this house, I reckon. There's a many things to see, when one's still but eight-and-twenty." She swayed her head slowly from side to side. "A many things to see and sorrow for."

I half suspected the old people were trying to enhance the spiritual terrors of their house by their droning insistence. I put down my empty glass on the table and looked about the room, and caught a glimpse of myself, abbreviated and broadened to an impossible sturdiness, in the queer old mirror at the end of the room. "Well," I said, "if I see anything to-night, I shall be so much the wiser. For I come to the business with an open mind."

"It's your own choosing," said the man with the withered arm once more.

I heard the faint sound of a stick and a shambling step on the flags in the passage outside. The door creaked on its hinges as a second old man entered, more bent, more wrinkled, more aged even than the first. He supported himself by the help of a crutch, his eyes were covered by a shade, and his lower lip, half averted, hung pale and pink from his decaying yellow teeth. He made straight for an armchair on the opposite side of the table, sat down clumsily, and began to cough. The man with the withered hand gave the newcomer a short glance of positive dislike; the old woman took no notice of his arrival, but remained with her eyes fixed steadily on the fire.

"I said—it's your own choosing," said the man with the withered hand, when the coughing had ceased for a while.

"It's my own choosing," I answered.

The man with the shade became aware of my presence for the first time, and threw his head back for a moment, and sidewise, to see me. I caught a momentary glimpse of his eyes, small and bright and inflamed. Then he began to cough and splutter again.

"Why don't you drink?" said the man with the withered arm, pushing the beer toward him. The man with the shade poured out a glassful with a shaking hand, that splashed half as much again on the deal table. A monstrous shadow of him crouched upon the wall, and mocked his action as he poured and drank. I must confess I had scarcely expected these grotesque custodians. There is, to my mind, something inhuman in senility, something crouching and atavistic; the human qualities seem to drop from old people insensibly day by day. The three of them made me feel uncomfortable with their gaunt silences, their bent carriage, their evident unfriendliness to me and to one another. And that night, perhaps, I was in the mood for uncomfortable impressions. I resolved to get away from their vague fore-shadowings of the evil things upstairs.

"If," said I, "you will show me to this haunted room of yours, I will make myself comfortable there."

The old man with the cough jerked his head back so suddenly that it startled me, and shot another glance of his red eyes at me from out of the darkness under the shade, but no one answered me. I waited a minute, glancing from one to the other. The old woman stared like a dead body, glaring into the fire with lack-lustre eyes.

"If," I said, a little louder, "if you will show me to this haunted room of yours, I will relieve you from the task of entertaining me."

"There's a candle on the slab outside the door," said the man with the withered hand, looking at my feet as he addressed me. "But if you go to the Red Room to-night—"

"This night of all nights!" said the old woman, softly.

"—You go alone."

"Very well," I answered, shortly, "and which way do I go?"

"You go along the passage for a bit," said he, nodding his head on his shoulder at the door, "until you come to a spiral staircase; and on the second landing is a door covered with green baize. Go through that, and down the long corridor to the end, and the Red Room is on your left up the steps."

"Have I got that right?" I said, and repeated his directions. He corrected me in one particular.

"And you are really going?" said the man with the shade,

looking at me again for the third time with that queer, unnatural tilting of the face.

"This night of all nights!" whispered the old woman.

"It is what I came for," I said, and moved toward the door. As I did so, the old man with the shade rose and staggered round the table, so as to be closer to the others and to the fire. At the door I turned and looked at them, and saw they were all close together, dark against the firelight, staring at me over their shoulders, with an intent expression on their ancient faces.

"Good-night," I said, setting the door open. "It's your own choosing," said the man with the withered arm.

I left the door wide open until the candle was well alight, and then I shut them in, and walked down the chilly, echoing passage.

I must confess that the oddness of these three old pensioners in whose charge her ladyship had left the castle, and the deep-toned, old-fashioned furniture of the housekeeper's room, in which they foregathered, had affected me curiously in spite of my effort to keep myself at a matter-of-fact phase. They seemed to belong to another age, an older age, an age when things spiritual were indeed to be feared, when common sense was uncommon, an age when omens and witches were credible, and ghosts beyond denying. Their very existence, thought I, is spectral; the cut of their clothing, fashions born in dead brains; the ornaments and conveniences in the room about them even are ghostly—the thoughts of vanished men, which still haunt rather than participate in the world of to-day. And the passage I was in, long and shadowy, with a film of moisture glistening on the wall, was as gaunt and cold as a thing that is dead and rigid. But with an effort I sent such thoughts to the right-about. The long, drafty subterranean passage was chilly and dusty, and my candle flared and made the shadows cower and quiver. The echoes rang up and down the spiral staircase, and a shadow came sweeping up after me, and another fled before me into the darkness overhead. I came to the wide landing and stopped there for a moment listening to a rustling that I fancied I heard creeping behind me, and then, satisfied of the absolute silence, pushed open the unwilling baize-covered door and stood in the silent corridor.

The effect was scarcely what I expected, for the moonlight, coming in by the great window on the grand staircase, picked out everything in vivid black shadow or reticulated silvery illumination. Everything seemed in its proper position; the house might have been deserted on the yesterday instead of twelve months ago. There were candles in the sockets of the sconces, and whatever dust had gathered on the carpets or upon the polished flooring was distributed so evenly as to be invisible in my candlelight. A waiting stillness was over everything. I was about to advance, and stopped abruptly. A bronze group stood upon the landing hidden from me by a corner of the wall; but its shadow fell with marvelous distinctness upon the white paneling, and gave me the impression of some one crouching to waylay me. The thing jumped upon my attention suddenly. I stood rigid for half a moment, perhaps. Then, with my hand in the pocket that held the revolver, I advanced, only to discover a Ganymede and

Eagle, glistening in the moonlight. That incident for a time restored my nerve, and a dim porcelain Chinaman on a buhl table, whose head rocked as I passed, scarcely startled me.

The door of the Red Room and the steps up to it were in a shadowy corner. I moved my candle from side to side in order to see clearly the nature of the recess in which I stood, before opening the door. Here it was, thought I, that my predecessor was found, and the memory of that story gave me a sudden twinge of apprehension. I glanced over my shoulder at the black Ganymede in the moonlight, and opened the door of the Red Room rather hastily, with my face half turned to the pallid silence of the corridor.

I entered, closed the door behind me at once, turned the key I found in the lock within, and stood with the candle held aloft surveying the scene of my vigil, the great Red Room of Lorraine Castle, in which the young Duke had died; or rather in which he had begun his dying, for he had opened the door and fallen headlong down the steps I had just ascended. That had been the end of his vigil, of his gallant attempt to conquer the ghostly tradition of the place, and never, I thought, had apoplexy better served the ends of superstition. There were other and older stories that clung to the room, back to the half-incredible beginning of it all, the tale of a timid wife and the tragic end that came to her husband's jest of frightening her. And looking round that huge shadowy room with its black window bays, its recesses and alcoves, its dusty brown-red hangings and dark gigantic furniture, one could well understand the legends that had sprouted in its black corners, its germinating darknesses. My candle was a little tongue of light in the vastness of the chamber; its rays failed to pierce to the opposite end of the room, and left an ocean of dull red mystery and suggestion, sentinel shadows and watching darknesses beyond its island of light. And the stillness of desolation brooded over it all.

I must confess some impalpable quality of that ancient room disturbed me. I tried to fight the feeling down. I resolved to make a systematic examination of the place, and so, by leaving nothing to the imagination, dispel the fanciful suggestions of the obscurity before they obtained a hold upon me. After satisfying myself of the fastening of the door, I began to walk round the room, peering round each article of furniture, tucking up the valances of the bed and opening its curtains wide. In one place there was a distinct echo to my footsteps, the noises I made seemed so little that they enhanced rather than broke the silence of the place. I pulled up the blinds and examined the fastenings of the several windows. Attracted by the fall of a particle of dust, I leaned forward and looked up the blackness of the wide chimney. Then, trying to preserve my scientific attitude of mind, I walked round and began tapping the oak paneling for any secret opening, but I desisted before reaching the alcove. I saw my face in a mirror—white.

There were two big mirrors in the room, each with a pair of sconces bearing candles, and on the mantelshelf, too, were candles in china candle-sticks. All these I lit one after the other. The fire was laid—an unexpected consideration from the old housekeeper—and I lit it, to keep down any disposition to shiver, and when it was burning well I stood round with my back to it and regarded the room again. I had pulled up a chintz-covered armchair and a table to form a kind of barricade before me. On this lay my revolver, ready to hand. My precise examination had done me a little good, but I still found the remoter darkness of the place and its perfect stillness too stimulating for the imagination. The echoing of the stir and crackling of the fire was no sort of comfort to me. The shadow in the alcove at the end of the room began to display that undefinable quality of a presence, that odd suggestion of a lurking living thing that comes so easily in silence and solitude. And to reassure myself, I walked with a candle into it and satisfied myself that there was nothing tangible there. I stood that candle upon the floor of the alcove and left it in that position.

By this time I was in a state of considerable nervous tension, although to my reason there was no adequate cause for my condition. My mind, however, was perfectly clear. I postulated quite unreservedly that nothing supernatural could happen, and to pass the time I began stringing some rhymes together, Ingoldsby fashion, concerning the original legend of the place. A few I spoke aloud, but the echoes were not pleasant* For the same reason I also abandoned, after a time, a conversation with myself upon the impossibility of ghosts and haunting. My mind reverted to the three old and distorted people downstairs, and I tried to keep it upon that topic.

The sombre reds and grays of the room troubled me; even with its seven candles the place was merely dim. The light in the alcove flaring in a draft, and the fire flickering, kept the shadows and penumbra perpetually shifting and stirring in a noiseless flighty dance. Casting about for a remedy, I recalled the wax candles I had seen in the corridor, and, with a slight effort, carrying a candle and leaving the door open, I walked out into the moonlight, and presently returned with as many as ten. These I put in the various knick-knacks of china with which the room was sparsely adorned, and lit and placed them where the shadows had lain deepest, some on the floor, some in the window recesses, arranging and rearranging them until at last my seventeen candles were so placed that not an inch of the room but had the direct light of at least one of them. It occurred to me that when the ghost came I could warn him not to trip over them. The room was now quite brightly illuminated. There was something very cheering and reassuring in these little silent streaming flames, and to notice their steady diminution of length offered me an occupation and gave me a reassuring sense of the passage of time.

Even with that, however, the brooding expectation of the vigil weighed heavily enough upon me. I stood watching the minute hand of my watch creep towards midnight.

Then something happened in the alcove. I did not see the candle go out, I simply turned and saw that the darkness was there, as one might start and see the unexpected presence of a stranger. The black shadow had sprung back to its place. "By Jove," said I aloud, recovering from my surprise, "that draft's a strong one;" and taking the matchbox from the table, I walked across the room in a leisurely manner to relight the corner again. My first match would not strike, and as I succeeded with the second, something seemed to blink on the wall before me. I turned my head involuntarily and saw that the two candles on the little table by the fireplace were extinguished. I rose at once to my feet.

"Odd," I said. "Did I do that myself in a flash of absent-mindedness?"

I walked back, relit one, and as I did so I saw the candle in the right sconce of one of the mirrors wink and go right out, and almost immediately its companion followed it. The flames vanished as if the wick had been suddenly nipped between a finger and thumb, leaving the wick neither glowing nor smoking, but black. While I stood gaping the candle at the foot of the bed went out, and the shadows seemed to take another step toward me.

"This won't do!" said I, and first one and then another candle on the mantelshelf followed.

"What's up?" I cried, with a queer high note getting into my voice somehow. At that the candle on the corner of the wardrobe went out, and the one I had relit in the alcove followed.

"Steady on!" I said, "those candles are wanted," speaking with a half-hysterical facetiousness, and scratching away at a match the while, "for the mantel candlesticks." My hands trembled so much that twice I missed the rough paper of the matchbox. As the mantel emerged from darkness again, two candles in the remoter end of the room were eclipsed. But with the same match I also relit the larger mirror candles, and those on the floor near the doorway, so that for the moment I seemed to gain on the extinctions. But then in a noiseless volley there vanished four lights at once in different corners of the room, and I struck another match in quivering haste, and stood hesitating whither to take it.

As I stood undecided, an invisible hand seemed to sweep out the two candles on the table. With a cry of terror I dashed at the alcove, then into the corner and then into the window, relighting three as two more vanished by the fireplace, and then, perceiving a better way, I dropped matches on the iron-bound deedbox in the corner, and caught up the bedroom candlestick. With this I avoided the delay of striking matches, but for all that the steady process of extinction went on, and the shadows I feared and fought against returned, and crept in upon me, first a step gained on this side of me, then on that. I was now almost frantic with the horror of the coming darkness, and my self-possession deserted me. I leaped panting from candle to candle in a vain struggle against that remorseless advance.

I bruised myself in the thigh against the table, I sent a chair headlong, I stumbled and fell and whisked the cloth from the table in my fall. My candle rolled away from me and I snatched another as I rose. Abruptly this was blown out as I swung it off the table by the wind of my sudden movement, and immediately the two remaining candles followed. But there was light still in the room, a red light, that streamed across the ceiling and staved off the shadows from me. The fire! Of course I could still thrust my candle between the bars and relight it.

I turned to where the flames were still dancing between the glowing coals and splashing red reflections upon the furniture; made two steps toward the grate, and incontinently the flames dwindled and vanished, the glow vanished, the reflections rushed together and disappeared, and as I thrust the candle between the bars darkness closed upon me like the shutting of an eye, wrapped about me in a stifling embrace, sealed my vision, and crushed the last vestiges of self-possession from my brain. And it was not only palpable darkness, but intolerable terror. The candle fell from my hands. I flung out my arms in a vain effort to thrust that ponderous blackness away from me, and lifting up my voice, screamed with all my might, once, twice, thrice. Then I think I must have staggered to my feet. I know I thought suddenly of the moonlit corridor, and with my head bowed and my arms over my face, made a stumbling run for the door.

But I had forgotten the exact position of the door, and I struck myself heavily against the corner of the bed. I staggered back, turned, and was either struck or struck myself against some other bulky furnishing. I have a vague memory of battering myself thus to and fro in the darkness, of a heavy blow at last upon my forehead, of a horrible sensation of falling that lasted an age, of my last frantic effort to keep my footing, and then I remember no more.

I opened my eyes in daylight. My head was roughly bandaged, and the man with the withered hand was watching my face. I looked about me trying to remember what had happened, and for a space I could not recollect.

I rolled my eyes into the corner and saw the old woman, no longer abstracted, no longer terrible, pouring out some drops of medicine from a little blue phial into a glass. "Where am I?" I said. "I seem to remember you, and yet I can not remember who you are."

They told me then, and I heard of the haunted Red Room as one who hears a tale. "We found you at dawn," said he, "and there was blood on your forehead and lips."

I wondered that I had ever disliked him. The three of them in the daylight seemed commonplace old folk enough. The man with the green shade had his head bent as one who sleeps.

It was very slowly I recovered the memory of my experience. "You believe now," said the old man with the withered hand, "that the room is haunted?" He spoke no longer as one who greets an intruder, but as one who condoles with a friend.

"Yes," said I, "the room is haunted."

"And you have seen it. And we who have been here all our lives have never set eyes upon it. Because we have never dared. Tell us, is it truly the old earl who—"

"No," said I, "it is not."

"I told you so," said the old lady, with the glass in her hand. "It is his poor young countess who was frightened—"

"It is not," I said. "There is neither ghost of earl nor ghost of countess in that room; there is no ghost there at all, but worse, far worse, something impalpable—"

"Well?" they said.

"The worst of all the things that haunt poor mortal men," said I; "and that is, in all its nakedness—'Fear!'

17

Fear that will not have light nor sound, that will not bear with reason, that deafens and darkens and overwhelms. It followed me through the corridor, it fought against me in the room—"

I stopped abruptly. There was an interval of silence. My hand went up to my bandages. "The candles went out one after another, and I fled—"

Then the man with the shade lifted his face sideways to see me and spoke.

"That is it," said he. "I knew that was it. A Power of Darkness. To put such a curse upon a home! It lurks there always. You can feel it even in the daytime, even of a bright summer's day, in the hangings, in the curtains, keeping behind you however you face about. In the dusk it creeps in the corridor and follows you, so that you dare not turn. It is even as you say. Fear itself is in that room. Black Fear.... And there it will be... so long as this house of sin endures."

FICTION

FICTION COLLECTIONS

NON-FICTION

Printed in Great Britain
by Amazon

79400259R00016